This book belongs to:

For Gran, with love ~ E.S.

Wish that I were a yellow bird,
I'd fly away with you,
But I am not a yellow bird,
So here I sit,
Nothing else to do.

First published in 2012 by Hodder Children's Books
This paperback edition published in 2013

Copyright © Ellie Sandall 2012

Hodder Children's Books
338 Euston Road
London, NW1 3BH

Hodder Children's Books Australia
Level 17/207 Kent Street
Sydney, NSW 2000

The right of Ellie Sandall to be identified as the author and illustrator of
this Work has been asserted by her in accordance with the Copyright,
Designs and Patents Act 1988.

ISBN: 978 1 444 93607 0

Printed in China

Hodder Children's Books is a division of Hachette Children's Books,
an Hachette UK Company

www.hachette.co.uk

COPYCAT BEAR!

Ellie Sandall

Hodder Children's Books

A division of Hachette Children's Books

Mango had a ginormous friend called Blue.

They went
everywhere together.

But there was a problem.
Blue copied **everything**
Mango did.

Mango flapped her wings.
Blue flapped his huge hairy paws.

Mango hopped along the ground.
Blue wobbled from one big paw to the other.

'COPYCAT BEAR!'
said Mango.

Mango flew up into a tree.
'Listen,' she chirped. 'You are a BEAR and I'm a BIRD.
Birds are different from bears. Birds live in trees!

'I do too,' said Blue.

And Blue climbed up
into the tree.

His big arms shook the branches and all the twigs
fell off Mango's new nest.

And with that she flew away.

Blue was all alone.

Mango swooped and soared
in the sunlight.

It felt strange to be on her own.
Then she flew down and sat
on a branch.

She started thinking about Blue.

Was he lonely by himself?

Was he thinking about her?

Evening came on and Mango flew off searching
everywhere for Blue.

She found him curled up under the tree where she'd left him.
'Birds are different from bears,' Mango said.
'But they can be best friends.'

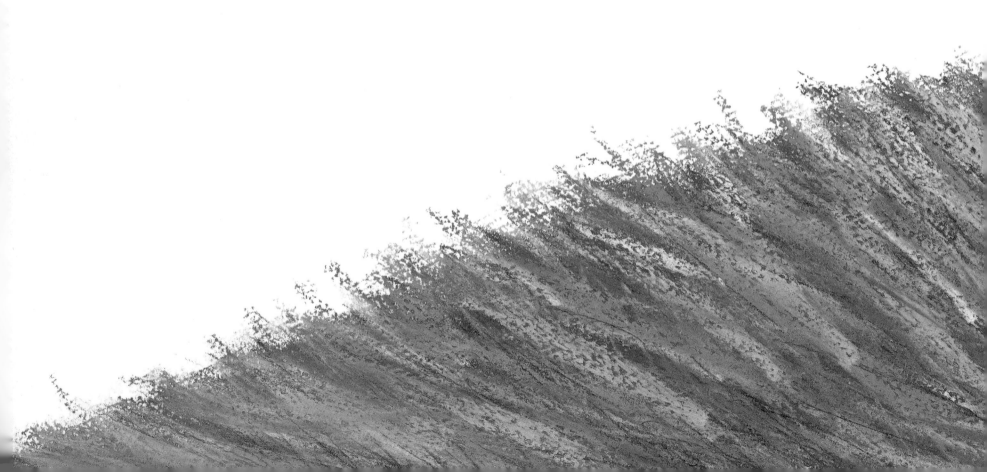

She hopped onto his broad back and snuggled into his thick fur.

'I missed you,' she sang softly.

'I missed you too!' said Blue.

'My Copycat Bear,'

said Mango happily.

If you enjoyed this book, you'll love...

WANTED: The Perfect Pet
'A hoot.' THE SUNDAY TIMES
Fiona Roberton
978 1 444 90263 1

STANLEY'S STICK
John Hegley
'...hours of imaginative play.' THE TIMES
illustrated by Neal Layton
978 0 340 98819 0

BABIES DON'T BITE
DAVID BEDFORD AND TOR FREEMAN
978 1 444 90353 9

For fun activities, further information and to order, visit:
www.hodderchildrens.co.uk

PITTIPAT'S SAUCER OF MOON
illustrated by Maria Nilsson
Geraldine McCaughrean
Purrfect for Bedtime!
978 1 444 90466 6

MIKI and the Moon Blossom
Stephen Mackey
978 0 340 95067 8